STEPHEN R. KING

Redstone

Crossroads IV

CROSSROADS SERIES: PART IV

Three more short stories from Stephen King's "Crossroads" series that will help keep you entertained late into the night. Discover the bright imagination, suspense, thrilling drama, picturesque visions, and a deeper look into the true landscape of the "Crossroads" series.

Follow the series to piece together the hidden meaning in the stories to determine the overall message that is being portrayed. Will it bring enlightenment? Will it be the light at the end of the tunnel? Does fear take over and leave the message hidden? The journey continues and the message will surely begin to appear and keep you in its grasp.

Copyright © 2014 by Stephen King

Manufactured in the United States of America
Designed by Magic Pen Designs

THE REDSTONE

Johan worked his field with the hoe in his hands. He was preparing to harvest his crops and bring his offering to the Autumn Festival. They only had a few weeks left so Johan was working his hardest to make sure everything was as ripe as possible before picking them.

His horse walked beside him with a large cart that Johan used to store his vegetables after picking them. Occasionally the horse would get distracted and Johan would have to return his attention to him with a carrot or two. It was worth it not to have to carry everything back himself. Every year that Johan did this he reminded himself that he should hire one of the local boys to come and work for him. He'd probably forget a week after the festival like always.

As Johan moved forward he looked up and saw that his horse had started moving away to go find some other food to snack on.

"Here boy!" Johan called. He picked a carrot from his bag and held it out to the horse. The horse smelled it and turned its head quickly. It looked hungrily at the carrot, despite the fact that Johan was sure he'd fed him at least six other carrots.

After the horse had sucked the carrot out of Johan's hand, he took his hat off to wipe his brow. When he looked towards the sun he saw a shape out on the hill. It looks a great deal like a dog. Johan wondered if one of the neighbor's dogs had gotten loose or simply wandered too far from home. Some people didn't keep their dogs within a fence. Johan didn't agree to that approach because the dogs upset the cattle and upset cattle meant a greater chance for poor meat, but to each their own he thought.

Then the dog howled. That was not the howl of a dog Johan recognized. He squinted and tried to look closer. It howled again and Johan felt fear crawl through him. He hoped it wasn't a wolf but he knew better. Sometimes they traveled a little too close to the farm. That meant that Johan was done for the day. He sighed and pulled his horse towards him.

"Come on. We gotta go back for now." The horse, who must have sensed his fear, easily complied. It was breathing heavily and would have probably run for it if Johan hadn't turned around.

Johan looked back and several other shadows had joined the one of the wolf up on the hill. Slowly, they began to advance down towards the farm. Johan turned and picked up the pace. The horse began to trot but it couldn't go any faster because of the cart tied to him.

Johan looked back again, afraid of what he might see. What he saw was a nightmare of machinery. The wolf was in fact made of metal limbs and tubes. Behind it were other monstrosities, all the various shapes and sizes. Johan ran as fast as he could, but he was no match for the nightmare that pursued him.

The swarm encased him, taking everything in his farm with it. When they'd passed through, nothing remained.

*****

The arrow struck the target with deadly force. A second arrow came seconds later and hit the center of the target, just millimeters beside the next one.

Jayna smiled and strung another arrow. She let it lose, piercing the first arrow straight down the middle. She smiled even brighter. The practicing she'd gotten recently had done wonders for her.

She stood in the field within the castle walls. Set inside those walls – at least a portion of it – had a practice area for the archers. Jayna was out there every day, shooting more and more arrows. The blacksmiths had made her a fresh batch of arrows, made with the purest of steel.

"Seems like you're doing well." said a friendly voice.

Jayna turned around. Cor'Vos was walking down the steps towards the archery range. He was dressed in his full Obsidian armor, the common garb of the Obsidian Knights. They were the king's premiere guard and were trained harder than any other soldier. Most of the time the knights were old and unable to travel. But Cor'Vos was one of the youngest Obsidian Knights. Because of this he was sent on different missions outside the kingdom constantly.

Jayna smiled and rushed over to him. She flung herself at him, wrapping her arms around him. "You're back!" Cor'Vos had been away on a mission for the King for the past few weeks. Since that time Jayna had missed him greatly.

Cor'Vos laughed and hugged her back. "And I'm not going anywhere for a while."

They broke apart and took stock of each other. Cor'Vos' long blonde hair had been trimmed slightly since the last time she saw him. His face also had some stubble growing on it.

Jayna on the other hand had let her hair continue to grow out. It was down past her shoulders now. She had it tied down at the bottom to keep it out of her face.

"You look good." Cor'Vos said, still smiling. He motioned to her ranger tunic. She'd received a new one after returning to the castle with Cor'Vos months ago. They'd just gotten back from saving the kingdom – more or less – from a deadly dragon. The king had seen fit to deem Jayna an honorary Obsidian Knight. Since then she'd been training hard to keep her skills sharp.

"Thanks." She said, beaming. "So do you. I like the stubble." She scratched at her nonexistent beard.

Cor'Vos laughed, scratching at it himself. "You do? Maybe I'll keep it for a bit."

"How did your errand go?" Jayna asked. They started walking down to the range. Jayna pulled her arrows out of the targets and put them in her quiver with the rest.

"Everything went fine." Cor'Vos said, resting his hand on his sword. "The travel was the worst part, but I'm getting better at these diplomatic missions." He smiled proudly.

Jayna stood up and slung the quiver over her shoulder. "Good. I'm glad you're making progress on that." She paused, "Any word on Solarn?"

Cor'Vos sighed. Solarn was a friend they'd lost during their last adventure. He was never found dead or anything. Instead he got lost in the End World during their battle with the Ender Dragon. Running out of time, Cor'Vos and Jayna were forced to close the portal. That left Solarn trapped in the End World. Any time that Cor'Vos and Jayna went traveling they'd ask around about him. They've yet to find any information on him. They'd pretty much given up hope that he'd found his way out.

"Well, we'll keep looking." Jayna said, trying to remain cheerful.

"How are you enjoying you're training?" Cor'Vos asked as they walked back to the armory.

"It's great! I do a lot of it on my own, but occasionally I get to train with the instructors." She said as she swung the armory door open.

Jayna stored her bow and quiver on a shelf. Cor'Vos took this time to remove his armor and store it inside the armory. Underneath he had on a cloth tunic. He shook his hair out, letting it go wild.

Jayna laughed at him and did the same. "You look ridiculous." She said.

Cor'Vos raised an eyebrow. "Well we can't all be as elegant as you." He cleared the hair from his face and put it all back in place behind him.

Jayna undid her tie and ran her fingers through her hair. It was freeing to not have it stuck behind her any longer. She laughed at Cor'Vos' comment. She really enjoyed having him back.

"I need to go report to the King soon." Cor'Vos said.

Jayna looked at him with surprise. "You haven't done that yet?"

Cor'Vos shook his head. "I came to see you first."

Jayna blushed and smiled. Then she reached out and nudged him. "You should go see him though. He's no doubt waiting for your report."

Cor'Vos nodded. "Yeah, probably." He hung his sword up near his armor. Then he turned back to Jayna. "Do you want to come with me?"

"Is that okay?" She asked.

Cor'Vos shrugged. "I don't see why not."

"Then sure." She followed him out of the armory and out into the practice area. They took the stairs back into the main castle. The inside was lit with torches, casting a bright glow within the stone hallways of the castle.

They made their way up to the throne room where two large Obsidian Knights stood guard. They bowed their heads as they approached.

"Sir Cor'Vos, Madam Jayna, welcome." They lifted their heads. "The King has been expecting you."

Cor'Vos nodded. "Yes. I'm here to deliver my report."

"Enter then." The guards stepped aside and the doors opened. The room past the doors was large and open. It was held up by great pillars, which were adorned with tapestries of the kingdom's greatest battles.

Cor'Vos and Jayna continued down the center of the room, towards the large throne that sat in the back of the room. Sitting on the throne was Malekeith, their king. He held a large staff in his hand and was flanked by two throne guards.

"Ah, Cor'Vos. You've returned at last." Said Malekeith. He stood and stepped towards the two. He left his staff in the hands of one of the guards. He came down the stairs and embraced Cor'Vos briefly.

Cor'Vos' cheeks burned with embarrassment. He enjoyed being in the King's favor, that was for sure, but he felt embarrassed about it being demonstrated in front of Jayna.

Then the King turned to her and bowed his head. "Lady Jayna, it's a pleasure to see you again."

Jayna bowed her head in respect. "And you to, your majesty."

"Come," said Malekeith as he went back up to his throne. "Tell me, Cor'Vos. How did your expedition go?"

Cor'Vos cleared his throat and began. "From what I found, there is a definite shortage of redstone in the neighboring kingdoms. Our joint investigations yielded no particular results. Just that they had been robbed and they'd been robbed quickly. Whoever took the redstone was able to move in out of the kingdoms undetected and very quickly. Considering large amounts of redstone are very heavy, we're looking at a large operation."

Malekeith nodded and stroked his beard. "Any idea who the culprit could be?"

Cor'Vos shook his head. "Bandits perhaps? But it seems unlikely because of the amount of redstone taken. It can't be any of the other kingdoms either because everyone has been robbed. They're all missing large quantities of the stuff."

Malekeith nodded thoughtfully. "Do you think it could be an outside force then? From across the sea?"

Cor'Vos sighed. "I'm not sure. I can't really say without more evidence."

Malekeith sighed as well. He seemed very tired. "Very well, I thank you for your service, Cor'Vos. I'm thinking we ne-"

BANG! The doors to the throne room slammed open. A man dressed in peasant garb rushed inside. The door guards were coming after him, trying to grab at his shoulders.

"What is the meaning of this?" Malekeith asked, standing. His voice was fierce and gave an air of dominance.

The guards finally grabbed hold of the man and held him back. "Urgent news, your highness! Your aid has been requested!" The man had clearly come from somewhere far and had been traveling nonstop. He was out of breath and looked like he hadn't eaten in days. His hair was thin and long and eyes bulged from their sockets.

He held a scroll in his hand, which was outstretched towards the king. Cor'Vos looked to Malekeith, who nodded. Cor'Vos took the scroll and handed it to the king. He opened it and scanned it with his eyes.

His expressions changed to a grave one. He looked over the scroll, down at the messenger. "You're sure?"

The messenger nodded. "It's a nightmare. They're everywhere. They're unstoppable. We need your help."

Malekeith took in a deep breath. "Very well!" He looked to Cor'Vos. "Take a battalion of troops and head out to the villages at once. Whatever's going on there needs to be stopped. If what's in here is true, then we need to cut the head off the snake before it grows." He leaned down and handed Cor'Vos the scroll. "Read this along the way. It might give you an idea of what you're facing.

Cor'Vos took it, but he was starting to become frightened based on the way Malekeith was reacting. He'd never seen the king act like that before. He stuffed the scroll in his belt and bowed.

"Of course, sir." Cor'Vos said. He stood up and passed Jayna a look of concern as they made their way out of the throne room. The messenger followed them out.

"So you'll help us?" He asked. His body was still shaking and his eyes darting from side to side. Whatever he saw will likely haunt him for years, Cor'Vos thought.

Cor'Vos turned back to him and nodded. "Yes. Return to your people, tell them to hide, get to somewhere safe. We'll be there as soon as we can."

A smile lit up the man's face, though it also highlighted his gaunt features. "Thank you." He took Cor'Vos' hand and shook his quickly. Then he took off past the two.

Jayna gave a large sigh. "I wonder what this is all about…" They walked silently for a few minutes before Jayna spoke again.

"I thought you said your missions were politically based." she said, sounding slightly offended.

Cor'Vos' cheeks burned. "Technically they were. A lot of the neighboring kingdoms were worried about their supply of redstone and what happened to it all. It's fairly clear that whatever they had was stolen. This is a different case than what happened to the last kingdoms that had their stuff go missing."

"In what way?" Jayna asked as they walked.

The halls of the castle were eerily empty, which made them silent. Cor'Vos wasn't used to them like this. He wondered absently if it was a sign of what was to come. "I have a feeling that everyone just gave their redstone away."

Jayna raised an eyebrow. "Why would they do that?"

Cor'Vos gave her a sly look. They'd nearly reached the barracks, which meant this conversation would be over shortly. "They might not want to admit it, but I think one of two things happened. Either they were forced to give it up, or they were swindled out of it. I have a feeling that it was the former."

"What gives you that impression?" Jayna asked. It sounded like Cor'Vos was making a lot of assumptions right now.

"All of the officials were being real cagey with me." He said as they walked down the steps towards the outside courtyard. "They were avoiding a lot of my questions and doing their best to distract me. This doesn't make sense because they were the ones who reached out to us for help in the first place."

"Do you think they were doing that just to save face?" Jayna asked.

Cor'Vos shrugged. "I'd like to think so, but I can't be certain just yet. It's all a bit muddled and confusing. But I guess it will have to wait for now." They'd just about reached the barracks.

Cor'Vos opened the wooden door and held it open for Jayna as they walked in. The quartermaster was inside with some of the other troops. They looked like they were busy cleaning their equipment when they entered.

The quartermaster turned and saw them. He immediately bowed. "Welcome, sirs."

Cor'Vos smiled. "The pleasure is mine. We need your help though."

The quartermaster stood immediately. "Absolutely. Anything you require, sir."

"We've been called to aid the neighboring villages. I'm not sure what's out there yet, but by the look on the messenger's face, we're dealing with something nasty. So make sure you guys bring your best stuff. You might need it."

The men stood at once and saluted. There looked to be about thirty men altogether. Cor'Vos wasn't sure that would be enough, but he also had no idea what they were up against. He didn't want to waste valuable time and resources, but he also didn't want to be outnumbered.

"Do you think this is enough?" Cor'Vos asked Jayna as the troops began to armor up and gather their things.

"I'll be honest with you." Jayna started. "I have no idea. I don't know what's out there. I'm just in the dark as you."

Cor'Vos rubbed his eyes. "I know that. But when the King gets frightened by something, you tend to notice."

Jayna nodded in agreement. "Yeah I did see that." She gave a sigh and went for her bow. "If he's able to go toe to toe with the Ender Dragon and not be afraid I'm shuddering to think what's got him concerned."

Cor'Vos threw his hands in the air. "Now you understand how I feel." He went over to the shelves and pulled off his sword. His suit of armor was kept in a coffin looking case nearby. It was of an omen, he thought. He hoped that it wasn't one he'd fulfill.

After he was dressed for battle he met the rest of the troops outside the barracks. Jayna was already there, her arrows slung around her shoulder and her bow in her arms.

The quartermaster approached Cor'Vos. "Do you want me to join you?"

Cor'Vos shook his head. "That won't be necessary. Thank you though. Stay back and prepare additional troops just in case I send word."

The quartermaster bowed his head and disappeared back into the barracks. Cor'Vos didn't feel the need to address his troops just yet, as he'd just talked to them. So instead he motioned towards the stables. The villages were a ways out and the horses would get them there as fast as possible.

Cor'Vos, Jayna, and their troops gathered their horses, saddled them, and tied their equipment to them.

"Everyone ready?" Cor'Vos asked. When he got the all clear he jumped up onto his horse. When he was ready he looked over at Jayna. She smiled and nodded to him. The rest of the troops boarded their horses and followed him out of the castle and into the wilderness.

The ride to the villages wasn't nearly as long as Cor'Vos thought it would be. In fact they reached the wreckage fairly quickly. The villages houses had their roofs burnt down and the stone foundations were crumbled. If people had lived here at any point there was no trace of them.

Cor'Vos dismounted his horse and looked around the village. He took out the scroll and reread it again, trying to look for any sign of what the letter described. It told of monstrous creatures surrounded by metal. They had nasty claws and howled like wolves.

As he walked he could see the claw marks in the stone. They were long and deep, clearly something rather strong had made them. But that was the only animal type mark on the battlefield. Everything else looked like it was burnt to the ground. There were black marks all over the landscape.

Jayna stepped beside him atop her horse. "What do you think?"

He sighed and kneeled down to examine a pair of claw marks on a piece of stone. "I have no idea. The letter describes wolf like monsters. The claw marks are rather strong all things considered, but everything else is consistent with a creeper attack."

Jayna looked around. "It seems kind of large scale for a creeper attack. Plus most people – even villagers – know how to defend against a creeper attack. Plus… where are the bodies?" She asked that last part in a near whisper.

Cor'Vos was himself was distressed about that as well. He stood, "I wish I knew." He walked back over to his troops. "Fan out! See if you can find anything interesting or out of the ordinary."

The soldiers did as they were told and started searching the area. Jayna joined Cor'Vos on foot and helped him cover the more immediate area.

"Where do you think the bodies could have gone?" Cor'Vos asked as they walked.

Jayna shrugged. "Beats me. If they were creepers though, which it doesn't seem like they are, then I would say they took them."

Cor'Vos nodded. He noticed the distinct lack of any footprints or handprints. There was no sign that human life ever existed here. "Why would they take them then? What purpose would the bodies serve?"

Jayna took in a breath. "I'm not sure. Maybe it's a religious thing. Another cult?"

Cor'Vos rolled his eyes. "I sure hope not. One dragon was enough. I don't want anyone summoning the end of the world again."

Jayna giggled and nodded in agreement. "I hear you on that one."

"Sir! Over here!" one of the soldiers called.

Cor'Vos and Jayna rushed over, along with the rest of the company. A pair of soldiers was standing over a pile of weird rubble. There were large tubes that were black and dripped a strange fluid.

"Is that oil?" Cor'Vos asked as he kneeled down.

None of the soldiers answered. Cor'Vos looked around at them and they all appeared clueless.

"We were afraid to touch it." One of the soldiers volunteered.

Cor'Vos nodded and looked down at the strange substance. It could have been oil, or some sort of tar. But he himself didn't want to touch it either.

He looked up at Jayna. "Can I borrow an arrow?"

Jayna slid one out of her arrows and handed it to Cor'Vos. He took it and dipped it in the liquid. He swirled it around and saw that it was much thicker than he expected. "This can't be oil. Maybe some kind of tar?" He looked up at Jayna. She made a face and shrugged.

Cor'Vos wiped the arrow on the ground and handed it back to Jayna. When he stood he noticed that there was a trail of the stuff that led on beyond the village limits. He turned back to Jayna, distressed.

"We need to move, now!" He called to his men. Everyone ran back to their horses and mounted them quickly. Cor'Vos brought his horse up towards the trail.

"They've moved on!" He called. "Possibly to another village. We need to move as fast as we can." Lowering his voice, he approached Jayna. "I need to you keep us on the trail. Can you do that as we move quickly?"

Jayna nodded. "I'll do my best."

Cor'Vos smiled. "That's all I ask." He pulled on the straps of his horse and led it up to the front of the battalion. Jayna took up a position just ahead of him. A moment later she'd picked up the trail and started forward. Cor'Vos motioned to the rest of the troops and they followed close behind her.

Cor'Vos was beginning to feel some nervousness growing inside of him. After seeing what they found at the village he truly had no idea what they were up against. At least when he went against the dragon he had a folk tale to go off of. This time though… there was nothing. The scroll had some information on it, but what they saw here at the village told a completely different story.

What would he do when they got there? Would it possible for them to face this threat with the weapons they had? These thoughts and more ran through Cor'Vos head as he followed Jayna through the wilderness.

He wondered how far this trail went. How far did these creatures go? Why were they attacking villages? How did they know where everything was? Was someone leading them? What was the tar all about?

At some point Cor'Vos had to try and shut out the questions. He had to focus and prepare for the potential of battle.

It was clear they had arrived by the towers of flame in the distance. And judging by the noise, the battle was still raging on.

Jayna pulled back next to Cor'Vos. "What do we do?"

"We have our orders." Cor'Vos said, attempting to sound confident. He drew his sword. Seconds later he heard the soldiers behind him follow suit. They rode towards the villages, their horses trampling the ground beneath them.

Cor'Vos could feel the heat of the fire against his face. He blinked away the sweat that was dripping from his forehead and tried to clear his mind. The worst thing he could do for him and his troops was be afraid even before things began.

But what he saw was something entirely unexpected. There were wolves alright…at least that's what they looked like from afar. As Cor'Vos neared them he saw that instead of fur their coats were made of metal and their claws were long and sharp. Tubes protruded from them in all manners.

Cor'Vos' eyes widened. The villagers screamed in terror and attempted to run for their lives. Many were unsuccessful as their cries attracted the attention of the monsters. They seemed determined to make sure no one escaped.

He tightened the grip on his sword and swung as hard as possible. It cut cleanly through the metal of the wolf's coat, cleaving it in two. He hoped the rest of the battle would be just as easy.

The wolves must have noticed that more people had entered because one of them howled – the alpha, Cor'Vos assumed – and attracted the attention of the others. They all came to their leader's side and went after the soldiers. They moved with lightning speed, almost unable to be seen as they ran.

The wolves seemed to completely ignore the horses. Instead they launched themselves over them, tackling the soldiers clean off their horses. Many of them flailed their arms, trying to grasp for their weapon.

Cor'Vos and Jayna dismounted before the wolves could take them. Cor'Vos tried to get his bearings and took stock of the battlefield. The wolves were focusing mostly on the soldiers now. Many of the villagers had been able to make a run for it thankfully.

Cor'Vos took his blade and did his best to free the soldiers from the wolves attacking them. In many cases though, he was too late. They'd already been killed.

Some of the soldiers had managed to free themselves and were now working to free their brothers in arms.

"Sir!" one of the soldiers called out to Cor'Vos. It was so loud that he couldn't place exactly where it came from. He turned wildly in order to find who was yelling at him.

"Our weapons don't work!" he said. "Their metal is too strong!"

Cor'Vos wasn't sure what he meant. His weapons were working just fine. Even Jayna's arrows were working fine against the wolves. But then he realized that he and Jayna were edge cases. They were Obsidian Knights and therefore their weapons were made differently than the regular soldiers. The iron was standard, but he never thought that it wouldn't work against these things.

He looked for Jayna, who seemed to be holding her own against the wolves just fine, but he was losing soldiers... and fast. There seemed to be an infinite number of them.

"We need to retreat!" he called out. He tried to move back to his horse, but many of them – including his own – had either run away or been killed in the crossfire.

Suddenly he was on the ground. The wind was knocked out of him and he couldn't breathe. His vision was blurred, but he could feel something heavy on him. Probably a wolf. It was clawing at him, but his armor held strong.

It was breathing heavily, but it sounded vaguely human. He wished his vision would clear so he could see properly.

His hands grasped at the dirt around him and he realized that his sword had left him. He had no idea where it was and he doubted that he could lift the wolf on his own. Cor'Vos was suddenly very thankful that his armor was made of one of the strongest substances on earth.

Cor'Vos could finally see again and saw something through all the metal and tubes. It almost looked human. Maybe female? Cor'Vos squinted to try and focus past all the coating.

Then he saw it. Through everything he locked eyes with a human girl. He couldn't tell much else about her, but judging by the shape of her face he definitely thought there was a female inside.

"Help me…" she asked in almost a whisper.

His eyes went wide. He struggled to find the words to say, but then the survival instinct kicked in. "Leave us and I'll try."

"I can't. He won't let me." The person inside the wolf said.

"I can't help you if you kill me." Cor'Vos said.

He finally seemed to get through. The wolf howled and he felt the crushing weight of its body release him. He sat up and saw that the pack was leaving. He wasn't sure where they were headed, but it didn't seem to be in the direction the villagers ran.

The girl who attacked him must have been the alpha wolf, Cor'Vos realized. He stood and looked around at the battlefield. It was strewn with bodies, almost all his soldiers. Jayna was standing a few feet away from him. Her hair was frazzled and she was covered in tar.

"Are you alright?" he asked, approaching her carefully.

She nodded, but remained silent.

The remaining troops gathered around him. They looked crushed. They'd never lost a battle so badly before.

"Where did they go?" one of them asked.

Cor'Vos shrugged. "I have no idea. Maybe they got scared?" He slowly approached one of the other wolf bodies and flipped it over. He knelt down and examined it. As far as he could tell, there wasn't anyone stuck inside. Was it the only the alpha who was like that? Were there other packs led by a similar alpha?

"What are you looking for?" Jayna asked, approaching him from the side.

Cor'Vos stood and looked for any remaining horses. Barely a few remained. Definitely not enough for the troops that were still here.

"Gather the horses." He ordered. "Pile on some of the bodies. We'll bring them back for study."

"We're heading home?" One of the troops asked.

Cor'Vos looked at him. The soldier was covered in dirt and blood. Cor'Vos offered him a kind smile and put a hand on his armored shoulder. "Yes. We're heading back. Gather as many supplies as you can and tie them to the horses. We'll need everything we can get our hands on for the journey back."

"What's our plan?" Jayna asked.

The soldiers left them to gather the horses and shove the bodies of the wolves onto the remaining horses. The soldiers also gathered up any armor and weapons they could find and bagged them on the horses' saddles.

"We'll head to the nearest village and hope that they haven't been hit by whatever this was." Cor'Vos said.

"Then we'll head back to the castle?" Jayna said. She sounded tired. Her walk was slow and her shoulders were hunched over.

The soldiers had finished gathering their things and had joined them on the trail towards the next village.

Cor'Vos nodded. "Yes. We need to tell the king about everything."

"What did you see out there?" She asked in a hushed whisper.

He looked over his shoulder. The soldiers weren't paying attention to them. They were just staring ahead, ignoring each other and everything else around them. He turned back to Jayna. "There was someone inside the alpha wolf." He said as plainly as possible.

Jayna blinked and raised an eyebrow. "What are you talking about?"

"When the alpha wolf attacked me, it had knocked me down and was trying to attack me." Cor'Vos said. "At one point I noticed there was someone inside there. A young woman. She asked for my help."

"Are you sure you weren't just seeing things?" Jayna asked him.

Cor'Vos grinned, but shook his head. "I spoke to her. I told her I would try if she let us live. Then the wolves just left. Something like that doesn't just happen on accident."

Jayna sighed. "So what are you thinking? That there are people inside these things?"

"Not exactly. I checked the others, only the alpha seemed to have a human body. The ones we have on the horses are just some kind of machinery."

"What do you think brought them here?" Jayna said as they walked.

Cor'Vos didn't have the slightest clue and he told her as much. "I wonder if this is somehow connected to the redstone shortages."

"Why would you think that?"

Cor'Vos cleared his throat. "I just think the timing is all rather convenient, that's all. All of this happening at the same time? It can't be an accident."

Jayna nodded. "I wonder what the scientists will think of all this when we get these things back to them."

Cor'Vos looked back at the horses carrying the wolves. "I can only hope that they'll be able to give us some answers."

The rest of the walk was silent as they marched towards the next village. It took them past nightfall to reach it and when they did they were lucky to find someone standing watch.

Cor'Vos waved as they approached. The watchman waved back and ran over to them.

"Boy am I glad to see you guys." He said. "We didn't think you'd make it out alive."

Cor'Vos gave him a questioning look. "What do you mean?"

He motioned back to the village. "We've got refugees from the other village. They told us what had happened. How did you make it out?"

Cor'Vos and Jayna exchanged an awkward glance. "It's complicated. May we stay the night though? Most of our horses were killed and we've been walking all day." If he really wanted to, Cor'Vos could pull rank as an Obsidian Knight, but he preferred not to if it wasn't necessary.

The watchman nodded gleefully. "Of course! Come on in. We've got plenty of room and we have horses you can use to get back to the castle tomorrow. I'm sure you need to get back there as soon as possible." He waved them forward and led them towards the village gates.

"You have no idea." Cor'Vos said with a wry smile as he followed the watchman. They were able to store the horses in the stables and wrapped the wolf bodies in large clothes to keep them hidden.

"Do you think that will work?" Jayna asked as they were finishing up.

Cor'Vos shrugged. "I certainly hope so."

They finished up and left the barn. The troops had already made their way into the inn. Cor'Vos said he would help keep watch with the village watchmen in return for letting them stay the night.

"I'll stay with you. It's only fair." Jayna said with a small smile.

Cor'Vos returned the smile and walked with her over to the village gates. The watchmen gave them each a cup and poured some liquid into it.

"It'll help keep you warm." The man said as he filled up everyone's cup.

Cor'Vos took a sip. It was a sweet tasting liquid, almost like chocolate. But it had a slightly saltier taste to it. He liked it. "Thank you." He said.

The night was cool, and there was a small breeze. It was a welcome change to the heat of battle, especially since he was still dressed in his armor.

Jayna came up beside him and nudged him. She smiled, holding a cup in her hands. "How are you feeling?"

He shrugged, but returned her smile. "I'm not really sure how to feel. I can't believe we nearly got killed today." He took in a deep breath. "I mean, we faced off against a dragon and came out alive. How did these 'wolves' or whatever they are, tear us apart?"

Jayna made a face and nodded. "I know what you mean. We lost a lot of good people today. But we'll get through this. If we can figure out how to get through a dragon and expel a religious deity, we can get through this."

Cor'Vos smiled. "You're right." He let out a sigh. "We just need to get back home."

The night passed silently, which Cor'Vos was thankful for. He'd had enough battle for one day.

The next morning, he awoke beside a lit fire. The sun was up and the watchmen had changed to different people. The shifts must have changed at some point. He looked over and saw Jayna resting beside him.

"You guys didn't last long." One of the watchmen commented.

Cor'Vos sat up and stretched out his limbs. Sleeping in armor was not his brightest idea. But frankly he didn't even remember falling asleep. He must have been truly exhausted.

Cor'Vos flashed the watchman a kind smile and stood. After stretching again for a moment he knelt down and woke Jayna.

"Why is the sun up?" She said in a sleepy tone.

Cor'Vos laughed. "We fell asleep. It's time we head out though." He helped her to her feet. She stumbled a bit and took a moment to focus.

"Okay." She said through a yawn. "I'm good. I'm good."

Cor'Vos smiled. "Come on, let's go get our guys." He took her by the hand and walked with her over to the inn. The breeze had remained, which Cor'Vos enjoyed. But he was beginning to feel a little stiff inside his armor. He was really looking forward to getting home and getting his armor off.

The troops were already eating their way through the inn's kitchen. The chef looked somewhat stressed as she ran around.

The troops noticed Cor'Vos and Jayna enter and stood to attention immediately. Many of them still had food in their mouths.

"At ease soldiers. Finish your meals quickly, we're heading out soon." He said.

The chef gave an audible sigh of relief. Cor'Vos and Jayna laughed and had a breakfast of their own. But they made it small in order to save the chef's sanity.

The pair enjoyed their warm meal of meats and eggs. When it was over the entire company gathered their things, thanked the chef for all her hard work and left.

They visited the stables and picked up their horses. This time they had enough horses to get everyone home. They tied the wolf bodies across their laps so they could carry them easily.

Before they left Cor'Vos made sure to thank the watchmen yet again for keeping an eye on them during the night and letting them stay in their village.

"It's our pleasure. Thank you for everything you do." The man at the gate said to him as they passed through. "Be safe on your way back to the castle."

Cor'Vos nodded. "We'll do our best."

The journey home was a quick one, which everyone was thankful for. Cor'Vos especially wanted to get home so he could finally get this armor off. But he knew that as soon as he got back there'd be more important things to do.

They immediately took the bodies of the wolves to the redstone tower. When they rode up, there was a guard at the front.

"Bring down the scientists." Cor'Vos said. The guard cast them a confused glance, but followed his orders quickly.

Moments later the redstone scientists had arrived down from their tower. They were all wearing white robes and were immaculately clean despite all the experiments and research they do.

"What are these?" They asked in near unison as they looked at the wolves.

"They're the wolves that attacked the villages." Cor'Vos told them. "I need you to take these and find out anything you can about them. It's crucial to the safety of the kingdom that you do this as fast as you can." Cor'Vos sat atop his horse and watched them as they listened to every word he said.

"Of course." They said. They called upon a couple of initiates. A few small bodied people dressed in similar robes rushed out of the tower and gathered up the wolf bodies. They carried them inside the tower and disappeared.

"We'll get you something as soon as we can." One of the scientists remarked before disappearing into the tower right behind his initiates.

That was one thing down. The next thing on Cor'Vos' to do list was to store the horses. Jayna, Cor'Vos, and the other soldiers took the horses to the stables. It was then that he dismissed the rest of the troops. They saluted and thanked him and went on their way.

"So what now? Are we done?" Jayna asked. She sounded exhausted.

Cor'Vos smiled. "I wish. We still have to brief in the king on what we saw."

Jayna sighed. "Do I have to go?"

Cor'Vos raised an eyebrow. "He probably expects you to be there."

She nodded. "Alright. Let's get this over with then."

They made their way over to the throne room. The guards let them in immediately. The king was already there, waiting for them. It was like he never left his throne. It amazed Cor'Vos that he was always waiting for them.

"Please! Come close. I've been waiting for you to return." Malekeith said.

Cor'Vos and Jayna stepped up to the throne and bowed.

"Rise. Tell me, what happened at the villages." The king was clearly distressed.

So Cor'Vos and Jayna relayed their tale of combat and mystery to Malekeith. He listened intensely, hanging on their every word. Occasionally he would tug at his beard and nod. He asked the most questions when Cor'Vos explained the bit about the alpha wolf. The idea that there was the potential to reason with them intrigued him.

"Maybe we could use that to our advantage. Do you believe that's possible?" He asked Cor'Vos.

"I certainly hope so, sir." Cor'Vos remarked.

"What curious monsters. You've already delivered them to the tower I assume?"

"Yes, sir. The scientists are very hard at work already." Cor'Vos told him.

"Excellent. But even so, there's no idea who is behind all this?" Malekeith asked.

Cor'Vos shook his head. "No idea. There were no emblems or coat of arms on anything we saw. Even the alpha wolf had no markings. And she didn't say anything about who was controlling them. But whoever it was clearly scared her."

Malekeith stroked his beard and stared thoughtfully into the throne room. "I don't suppose you know of any way to track them?"

Cor'Vos deferred to Jayna for this one. "I'm not entirely sure. One of them must have gotten injured because I was able to track it through its… 'blood' or something. I'm honestly not sure what it is."

The king nodded, taking everything in. "So we really don't know where they are right now? I am correct in assuming that?"

Both Jayna and Cor'Vos nodded. The king sat back and sighed. "Perfect." He took another moment to think before lifting his head again. "Thank you for everything you did. Both of you. You're dismissed. I'll summon you again when the scientists find something."

Cor'Vos and Jayna bowed and turned to leave the throne room. When they exited Cor'Vos let out a long sigh. "I'm glad that's over. I expected him to be angrier for some reason."

Jayna nodded in agreement. "He just seems tired."

"He's been king for a long time." Cor'Vos commented. "I wonder what will happen when he decides it's time to give up the throne."

Jayna nudged him in the shoulder. "Maybe he'll make you king."

Cor'Vos rolled his eyes and started for the barracks. "I somehow doubt that. I don't know the first thing about ruling."

"But you did kill a dragon." She said as she followed him. "That's got to count for something."

Cor'Vos shrugged. "I think it did. But I don't need to be king in exchange. I'd rather be out in the field whenever possible. I don't think I could stand only hearing about things and not knowing what's going on out there."

Cor'Vos opened the door to the barracks and found his troops eating yet again inside. They saluted casually and went on with their day. Cor'Vos returned the salute and took off his armor.

The relief he felt after being out of the obsidian cage was amazing. He was able to stretch out his limbs and try to get out all the knots he'd created by being in there for too long.

"What's next?" Jayna asked.

Cor'Vos finished his stretching and returned to standing straight. He groaned and massaged his shoulder.

"We wait." He said. "There's nothing we can do until the scientists come back with something for us. That or we wait for another attack to happen. There's no predicting where these guys will hit next, so we can't even fortify properly."

Jayna nodded. "So we're just staying in for now?"

Cor'Vos shrugged. "More or less. We don't have a choice."

So days passed on quietly at the castle. Cor'Vos checked in several times a day with the redstone scientists to see if they had found anything. More often than not they'd have nothing. They simply didn't understand the creatures. Occasionally they'd make some kind of discovery but it wasn't of any major consequence. They were just excited to know *something* about these things.

It was also silent on the village front. There had been no new attacks or reports of anything happening. Cor'Vos had even got out there himself to make sure the villages hadn't been wiped out instead.

But no, they were still standing there when he arrived. He talked with the villagers and learned that they hadn't heard anything about these creatures since the last attack.

This troubled Cor'Vos. The threat clearly wasn't gone. But why hadn't they attacked? Did their one defeat force them into a retreat? Did they outright surrender when they left? What about the girl – the alpha wolf? Cor'Vos' head hurt when these questions swarmed his mind.

What troubled Cor'Vos even more was the site before him as he returned back to the castle. Smoke rose from the castle's entrance and shadows loomed. Rubble stood at the front of the castle. It looked like the gates had been blown down. As his horse galloped a strange shape came into view.

It looked like a castle with arms and legs. It looked to be made of the same materials as the wolves were. Wires and tubes ran throughout it. Cor'Vos could only assume that this is what had caused some of the destruction.

Dread ran through him. Was this what controlled the wolves? Is this what was causing all of the madness?

A loud voice answered the questions in his mind. "All those who follow Malekeith! Know that your neighbors have been slain! Their castles ruined! And their villages burned!"

Cor'Vos pulled back on the reins and waited. He didn't want to risk getting blown out of the sky by whatever giant contraption stood before him.

"I am giving you one chance! Surrender your king and I will spare your kingdom!" the voice called. "You have one day! Fail me, and I will unleash my hounds upon you all. Not one of you will survive!"

Then with that there was silence.

Cor'Vos was hesitant to approach the castle through the front so he moved his horse around the other side of the castle. There was a siege exit that was to be used to evacuate citizens in the event of a large scale battle. He imagined that this counted somehow.

He was right. By the time he made his way around the other side he could see the rocks already being moved by the castle guards. Perhaps this time they were opening it to evacuate the king instead of his people.

"Sir Cor'Vos!" one of the guards called as he approached. "The King wants to see you immediately!"

Cor'Vos thought he might. He dismounted and left his horse with one of the guards outside. He made his way through the tunnels as quickly as possible. He had never been down in the siege tunnel before, so he felt a bit disoriented as he ran.

Thankfully it was a straight path that led up to the main hall of the castle. Just ahead of him was the throne room. He could see the other throne guards speaking with Malekeith. It looked like there were some redstone scientists in there as well.

Jayna was already in there, pacing back and forth. When she saw him she ran and embraced him. "Are you okay?" She asked.

They pulled away from each other. Cor'Vos gave her a small smile. "I'm fine. I was doing some rounds on the outside villages. What happened here? What is that thing out there?"

"I was a fool." Malekeith said before Jayna could respond. He looked older, much older than the last time Cor'Vos had seen him. The bags under his eyes looked heavier, and his complexion was pale. He looked like he'd recently been running. He was breathing heavily and seemed very out of breath.

"What do you mean?" Cor'Vos asked him.

"We don't have much time." Malekeith said, motioning for Cor'Vos to come closer. "The man out there, his name is Lion. Mr. Lion." Malekeith coughed and tried to catch his breath.

"Sir, you need to leave now." One of the guards said.

Malekeith waved him off. "He was one of us. Years ago. He was a genius, one of the most talented scientists we had. It was because of him we were able to harness obsidian."

Malekeith gave off a heavy sigh. "But his talents got the better of him. He became dangerous, psychotic even, when it came to the experiments he ran. It got to the point where we had to exile him. Keeping him in prison never worked, he was too smart for us and always escaped. So we cast him out."

Cor'Vos cast Jayna a concerned glance. "What happened next?"

Malekeith looked like he was beginning to regain some of his color. His breath was returning to him. "He tried going to the neighboring kingdoms. But by then they'd heard about what he was trying to do. So he left. He took his daughter and went across the sea and set up shop outside of our jurisdiction."

"Now he's back for revenge I assume, and to prove us wrong for sending him away. I should have killed him when I had the chance, Cor'Vos... But I thought that mercy was the way to go." Malekeith let out a breath and Cor'Vos knew he was finished.

"We'll take care of it." He told the King. Cor'Vos then turned to the throne guard. "We need to give any available soldiers whatever obsidian weapons we have left. It's the only thing that works on those wolves."

"But those weapons are reserved strictly for Obsidian Knights." The guard argued.

Malekeith waved him aside. "Do what he says, soldier. He's fought the damn things. And if we don't hold them back it won't matter if there is any obsidian left or not."

The guard bowed his head and ran off without another word. Then one of the scientists stepped forward. "I might have good news." He said.

Cor'Vos felt the slightest glimmer of hope grow inside him. "What is it?"

The scientist cleared his throat. "We've been studying the wolves you brought us, disassembling them and getting any information we can from their bodies. What we eventually realized that they are a purely mechanical construct. And because of this, they cannot make their own decisions. There's a host of some sort, which we believe to be the alpha you referred to before."

Cor'Vos nodded. "Okay, but this is all stuff we knew already. What's the good news?"

The scientist looked mildly offended by Cor'Vos' comment, but decided to press on anyways. "You need to cut off the host. Take out the alpha and the rest will shut down."

Cor'Vos knew that as well. He was beginning to get frustrated. "Anything else?"

The scientist huffed. "Yes. If you'd just given me a moment I'd tell you. I came up with something to jam the signal with. It's temporary, because it requires charges made from the same material as the wolves themselves. If we had more wolves we could make it last longer." The scientist took the device from his pocket and handed it to Cor'Vos.

It was small, almost circular in shape. It had a reddish tinge to it that reminded Cor'Vos of brick. He took it and held it in his hand. It was extremely lightweight. He wondered absently how it worked.

"Unfortunately we don't have the luxury of obtaining more wolves." Cor'Vos said, pocketing the device in his bag.

"I thought not." The scientist replied.

"So what will we do now?" Jayna asked.

Cor'Vos didn't have the slightest idea. But he knew what he had to accomplish. "We need to get on that… ship?" He realized he didn't even know how to describe it. "If we do that, we can use this device to disable the wolves and then take out Mr. Lion."

Jayna nodded. "That definitely sounds easier said than done."

Cor'Vos chuckled. "For sure. But we don't have a choice. We can't win a full scale battle against these things." He turned back to the scientist. "How many charges does this thing have?"

The scientist looked grim. "We're not sure. It could have three, maybe four at most. Either way, I wouldn't use them lightly."

Cor'Vos didn't intend to. But in the event of an emergency, he wanted a way out. "Let's see if we can find a way into this thing."

Malekeith stood. "Best of luck to you both, and thank you." The guards then ushered him away, down the path through which Cor'Vos arrived before.

Cor'Vos turned to Jayna. "Ready?" He asked with a wry smile.

She returned the smile. "Let's do it."

They headed through another of the castle's many exits. This left them on the west side of the walls, putting them behind the great beast. Cor'Vos began to realize its true size as they approached. It was much larger up closer, as it was clearly made to house hundreds, if not thousands of wolves.

Thankfully it appeared no one was guarding the machine from any angle. They must have thought it to be impenetrable.

Hope filled Cor'Vos as he spotted a ladder near the one its legs. He assumed it was used for maintenance or some such work. There looked to be one on each leg.

He beckoned Jayna over and she ran to him as fast as possible. He hopped up on the ladder and climbed as fast as he could. Cor'Vos continued his climb until he reached the hatch at the top. He pulled the lever and pushed hard against the metal. It moved and flapped open. Cor'Vos smiled. Now they were getting somewhere.

The pair climbed inside, trying to make as little noise as possible. Jayna was able to move as silent as the night, but Cor'Vos' armor made it difficult for him to get around without making some noise. He thought about dumping it, but it was the only thing standing between him and the talons of the wolves.

The interior of the ship was bright red. The lights were bright and the place was covered in metal sheets. The thing was definitely pumping out a lot of heat because the temperature had risen considerably.

Once they were onboard their next step was to find the bridge. Cor'Vos thought of this as a ship. Operations were probably towards the front of the ship, and higher up than they were now.

"Over here." Jayna said, calling him over. She'd discovered the stairs to the next floor. Unfortunately for them, the wolves looked to be actively patrolling this floor. This was when Cor'Vos really began considering leaving his armor. He figured if they were caught, he'd be dead anyways.

But he just couldn't do it. Not yet at least. So they lumbered on. There looked to be about five wolves on this floor, all of which were patrolling in a set pattern. All they had to do was wait for their moment and get across as quickly as possible.

That was one floor down, but Cor'Vos had no idea how many they had left before reaching the bridge.

The next floor was larger and seemed to house a great deal of tubes and some kind of generator. Cor'Vos wasn't too familiar with redstone technology, so it all flew a bit over his head.

The problem here though, was that the room was far more open than the previous floor. The patrolling wolves would seem them easily. Cor'Vos and Jayna spent a minute trying to see if there were any other ways around, but there was nothing there to give them cover.

Cor'Vos sighed and pulled the device out of his bag. He glanced at Jayna, asking her silently if he should use it. She looked back up at the room, then back at Cor'Vos. She nodded.

He took in a deep breath and pressed the button in the center of the device. It began to glow and vibrate. Cor'Vos slid it on the ground into the center of the room. The noise level grew. Cor'Vos opened the hatch to the level below and told Jayna to get inside. He followed quickly behind her.

A moment later there was a muffled bang.

"Is that all?" Jayna asked.

Cor'Vos shrugged. "Let's hope so." He opened the hatch and peeked inside. All of the wolves were deactivated. Their bodies were limp, lying on the ground. He looked back down at Jayna. "We're good."

They climbed back up and made their way over to the generator. "This has got to be what powers the whole thing." Jayna said.

"Should we shut it down?" Cor'Vos asked.

"Then they'd know we were here." Jayna said.

Cor'Vos stared at the generator for another minute. He wanted to shut it off in case they weren't able to make it out alive, but if they were made then they certainly wouldn't get out alive. "You're right. We can't risk it just yet."

So instead the pair made their way over to the ladder and did the same thing over again. They carefully opened the hatch and peered inside. This time it was an empty level.

Despite there being nothing there, Cor'Vos did not feel at ease. There was something suspicious here. Perhaps this was a loading dock of some sort, or an area where deactivated wolves went to rest. Either way, it didn't make sense for there to be an empty level here.

"Cor'Vos look out!" Jayna yelled suddenly.

Before Cor'Vos had time to react there was a wolf on of top of him. He didn't even think; he just clicked the button in the center of the device. The pulse that went off knocked the wind out of him, but otherwise he was unharmed. The wolf had deactivated and Jayna helped him shove it onto the floor.

"Are you alright?" She asked in a hushed whisper. By now their entrance was probably known here, but it's worth hoping otherwise.

"I'm fine." He took her hand and stood up. "I wish I hadn't used another charge though. Now there's no telling if the thing will work." Cor'Vos stared at the device in his hand. He kicked himself for having to use it.

He sighed and stowed it in his bag and moved to the ladder. As they climbed he could hear footsteps above. He motioned to Jayna what he heard and she nodded. Together, they made their way inside.

This was it. This was the bridge. And like Cor'Vos thought, their presence was known. They were surrounded immediately by the wolves. From a distance Cor'Vos could see the larger one, the Alpha. A man stood near the cockpit, facing the window.

"I was wondering when Malekeith would send someone for me." The voice was different than Cor'Vos expected. The man certainly had a different accent, one never Cor'Vos had never heard. He assumed it was from wherever he'd been all this time.

"I should consider myself honored I guess, that he sent two Obsidian Knights for me." Mr. Lion turned and showed himself. He wore glasses and had a thin mustache with full head of greying hair. "Though during my time they didn't have women knights just yet."

Cor'Vos dropped his arm to his sword. "That won't be necessary." Mr. Lion stated, coming towards them. "I have no quarrel with you, just your king. I don't want to harm anyone else."

"You should tell that to the villagers you burned and mauled to death." Cor'Vos said with venom in his voice.

Mr. Lion shrugged. "Acceptable losses in my opinion. Plus I needed the organic material, so their lives were not wasted."

Cor'Vos knew the man was crazy, but this was a separate level altogether. "You're insane." He said.

Another shrug. "Perhaps. But that's not a reason to send a man from his home, the only one he's ever known. There are better ways to handle things than sending a man and his family to lawless lands across the sea."

That's when Cor'Vos remembered, Malekeith had mentioned a daughter of Mr. Lion's. He looked back at the Alpha and remembered the young woman he saw inside the cage of steel. The one who had asked for his help... and it all came together.

While Mr. Lion paced, Cor'Vos reached behind him, trying to pull the back closer to him. "So instead you turned your daughter into a monster?"

Mr. Lion barely cast her a glance. "I did what was necessary to protect us."

"You call terrorizing millions of people protecting?" Cor'Vos said, hoping the back and forth would provide as a decent enough distraction. His hand was in the bag now. All he had to do was grab the device and arm it. He hoped this wouldn't hurt the girl inside, but it was a risk he was willing to take in order to disable the entire army.

"I've only done what was necessary. Malekeith and the others deserved to know my pain. What happened across the sea..." Mr. Lion faced away from them entirely. "It was madness."

Cor'Vos finally gripped the device. He looked over at Jayna, who was ready to go at a moment's notice. He nodded and armed the device. He prayed that the device would actually discharge. He'd already used a few charges before, and if this didn't work they'd be dead in seconds.

"I'm sorry." Cor'Vos said to the girl. He took a deep breath.

"What?" Mr. Lion asked, turning around.

It was too late though. Cor'Vos threw the device as hard as he could towards the Alpha. Before anyone else could do anything about it, a loud bang went off and there was a flash of light.

For a moment Cor'Vos couldn't see or hear anything. His vision came back first and all that he saw was that all the wolves had collapsed. He saw Mr. Lion running for the console up front. He saw Jayna covering her ears, just getting her bearings back.

He still couldn't hear anything except a terrible ringing in his ears. Even so, he drew his sword and lumbered towards Mr. Lion. Whatever he was doing, he doubted it would be good.

A terrible lurching sent Cor'Vos off balance. He tumbled back on to the ground, unable to figure out what was going on. He managed to catch a glimpse of what was happening through the window and realized the machine was moving.

"Shoot him!" Cor'Vos called to Jayna. He couldn't see her. He just hoped that she was in a better spot than he was. The armor was heavy and keeping him from getting up as fast as he could look.

When he finally stood he saw Jayna moving towards the control panel. She had an arrow strung in her bow.

"Step away from the console!" She yelled.

Mr. Lion turned around and laughed. "It's too late now!" An arrow pierced his heart seconds later. He made a strange gurgling noise and tried to take a step forward. Jayna strung a second arrow and fired it. That put Mr. Lion to the ground.

Cor'Vos rushed over to the console and saw that no matter what he did, the machine wouldn't stop moving. If he didn't stop it soon then it would barrel through the gates and crush anything in its path.

"I can't stop it." Cor'Vos said, freaking out. They'd come so far only to fail now.

"What about the generator?" Jayna asked.

"Of course!" Cor'Vos said, rushing back to the ladder. Before he opened the hatch though he heard a noise. He looked over and saw the young woman stirring. She was alive!

He ran over to her and drew his sword. Carefully, he used it to cut through the steel and free her. He then sheathed it and picked her up in his arms. She was still a bit woozy, but she seemed to be okay otherwise. Quickly, they made their way back to the generator level.

"Any idea how to shut it off?" Cor'Vos asked. He had originally planned to use the device the scientists made, but it was out of charges.

"I'm sure the old-fashioned way would work just fine." Jayna said.

Cor'Vos nodded. A sword would always work… He hoped. He handed off the girl to Jayna. "Take her back to the castle. I'll take care of things here and follow behind you."

Jayna froze for a moment. "Are you sure?"

Cor'Vos was too busy staring at the generator to turn to her. "Yes. Don't worry."

"Okay." She said. "Be careful."

"I'll be there soon." Cor'Vos said. He waited until they left before drawing his sword. There really didn't seem to be a particular spot that looked weak enough or that would cut power. So he decided to just stab the thing in the center.

The sword entered with ease. The generator began to spark. Cor'Vos recoiled as to not get shocked. He figured that would do the trick, so he headed to the hatch.

But what he discovered immediately caused him panic. The hatch was closed as expected. But it wouldn't open. No matter how hard he pulled on it, the hatch refused to open.

Cor'Vos rushed back to the generator and tried to pull his sword out. It was stuck just as badly as the hatch was.

So now he was stuck in a large metal contraption that was on the verge of exploding. Perfect.

He tried to make his way up instead. But the hatch there was locked as well. Whatever he'd done to the generator, it was designed to seal the room if anything happened to it.

So he was stuck with literally no way out. Cor'Vos did his best to control his breathing. He'd been in life and death situations before, but there was always a chance he'd survive. Now he was sure that he would be dead any moment now.

What was one to do in this kind of situation? He could spend any remaining time he had left banging on the walls, hoping he could get through, but he knew that would never work.

So instead he did something he never thought he would do in a situation like this. He went into the corner of the room and curled up as well as he could. His best chance now was the armor he had wanted to dump so badly before the mission began. If anything was going to help him survive, it would be the obsidian armor.

He just hoped that-

BANG!

White light enveloped the room and Cor'Vos went blind.

The next thing Cor'Vos saw was Jayna's face above him. He couldn't hear anything just yet. But he could see her lips moving. She smiled and then looked behind her and said something to someone he couldn't see.

He felt his armor. There were definitely dents in it, but otherwise he seemed unharmed. He knew he'd be sore for weeks though.

"Can you hear me?" Jayna asked when she returned.

Her voice was muffled, but he could understand her well enough. He nodded. "Pretty much."

She smiled and helped him to a sitting position. He was outside the castle. He looked around and saw the debris of the giant machine a few yards away. His helmet lay next to him in the ground.

Cor'Vos blinked and stretched out his jaw. His ears popped and a barrage of sounds came rushing in.

"Are you okay?" Jayna asked, putting a hand on his shoulder.

Cor'Vos turned to her and smiled. "Yes, I think so."

"Can you stand?" She asked.

Cor'Vos hadn't even thought about his legs until she mentioned it. "Maybe?" He said with an awkward laugh. He couldn't really feel them, but he hoped it was just his body getting used to being awake again.

Carefully, she helped him to his feet. It was rough at first, and he definitely had to lean on Jayna for support. But he stabilized eventually.

"So it's over now?" She asked.

Cor'Vos nodded. "He's dead, the machine is destroyed, and the wolves are deactivated." He twisted his neck around slowly. "Speaking of which, where's the girl?" They turned and began walking back to the castle.

"She's with the redstone scientists right now. They think she'll be okay." Jayna said.

"Perfect. So everything worked out then." Cor'Vos said with a smile.

Jayna took his hand and gave it a warm squeeze. "Yes. But you need your rest. Come on."

Cor'Vos didn't argue. He let her help him back into the castle.

Our First Words

With a cough came Marie's first word, for a second we both looked at each other and at the thing that had hatched from her lips and fallen to the cobbles below.

Oh shit, I remember thinking and then somewhat guiltily, please God let it be a good one.

"What the hell are we going to do?" Marie said, her eyes wide.

The word fluttered ineffectually against the snow and slush. It was obvious that it was never going to survive in weather like this, what was I supposed to do? I scooped it up in the palm of my free hand, and held it cupped hand against my chest, hoping at least it would make the journey home.

"Sebastian…" Marie ran to catch up as I hurried on, her black storm-trooper boots sending sprays of dirty slush and wet behind her. "We can't do this. You know the price." She puts a hand out to my shoulder, the fingers that poked out of her worn gloves were too pale and too thin. "You know what comes next, right?"

"I know." I said, but what can you do?

*****

Later that evening in our small apartment we curled up on the floor and listened to the wheezes of an old building. The cold did more than frost the windows; it juddered down old pipes and whistled through the outside hallway. Between us and our small one-bar heater I made up a shoebox, stuffing it with the newspaper I usually reserved for the cracks under the doorframe and settled the word into it. Within seconds it had rustled and fluttered into its nest, wrapping its papery wings around itself until there was no sign of what it might read.

"This is a really stupid idea, you know that right?" Marie sat down next to me, her neon-blue hair making her only look thinner, a creature of the cold and winter.

"No it's not." I lied. "And anyway, I thought it was my stupid ideas you liked about me?"

"Not really." Marie said, leaning back against our worn out sofa, "it was probably your hair. You had great hair a year ago."

I feigned hurt, she laughed, and for a second we forgot about the shoebox filled with promise just at our feet. I flicked our old service radio on, letting it re-tune itself every few minutes to the nearest pirate radio frequency. Old time music faded in and out of the crackle and hiss of static. For the rest of the evening we carefully didn't talk about the word in the box by the fire, what it might read, what it meant for us, what would happen next. Occasionally, in between Bessie Smith and Marvyn Gaye we would hear its papery shivers as it nuzzled deep in its nest. We would look at each other for a moment, not saying anything.

I prayed that it would make it through the night. God alone knew what we would do then.

*****

The words were no great respecters of people. They ignore social standing, gender, health or money. No one knew who would get afflicted, or why. They would arrive in the middle of business meetings and amongst strangers. They would trip off the tongues of loved-ones halfway through dinner, splashing into the soup before they flew for the nearest window. They emerged in prisons, public parks, hospitals, between lovers curled up in their hideaways and amidst enemies sworn to fight. The process never hurt, there would just be the need to cough and suddenly, from nowhere out would fall this bundle of papery wings and color.

I was only a kid when the words first arrived. At first, they were called miracles. Even in these cold times people took to the streets, formed cults. Society was never the same again. Whole branches of linguistic theory opened up, Etymologists tried to capture the errant vocabularies with nets, before cataloguing and storing them in Kilner jars.

The scientists studied the words themselves. Did they have meaning? Were they trying to tell us something? Why was this happening? The words came in every language, in whatever the mother tongue was of the speaker. There were ordinary words like sink, house, weather, purple. There were extraordinary words like lepidoptery, sanguine, silicide, nefelibata. I remember seeing the 'words spotted' posters as the city was transformed into a grammarian heaven. On every street corner a list of the words seen in this vicinity, with space to scribble your own sightings.

Me and Marie were about nineteen, and still little more than street kids in the freezing city when we went to see our first word-flock. I knew a way to get up to the balcony of the domed museum-library where we could watch the big, iridescent clouds of words that used to swamp the city.

It was tough going, up on the icy rooftops in that cold, and Marie kept on slapping me for trying to make out with her.

"Why the hell would I want to catch frostbite for the likes of you?" She laughed.

But then we saw them. The green verdigris-roof was almost covered by the flock, their miniature wings flexing and twitching in the weak sunlight, flashing brilliant colors into the backs of our eyes.

Neither of us said anything as we waited in silence. Her hand found mine. There must have been ten thousand easily, maybe half a million words up here, trying to catch a bit of warmth.

Then, startled by some sharp sound of the city below, a ripple spread through the flock and seismically they took flight. The air was filled with scintillation, with purples, blues and greens. Flashes of silver and mauve and red as the flock broke apart, fragmented, atomized to the point that it seemed that they could never again be called whole. Magically they would reform, some inner current would pull them back together, contracting, joining up its verbs and adjectives together to form a complete horde. How many novels were in there? How many complete works of Shakespeare, Dickens, Mahabarata?

The word-flock flashed and trembled as it spread into the sky above the city, constantly roiling as it moved to find a quieter spot.

"Holy A!" Marie swore. We both stared at the cloud until it became nothing more than a shadow against the city skyline before allowing ourselves to breathe out. "Okay, that was worth the frostbite," she said, silencing whatever dumb thing was going to fall out of my mouth with our first kiss.

*****

But then later that same year the news got out: the speakers were dying.

They died after a second mysterious word-birth, soon to be known as the Last Word. Instead of being classified as wonders of nature and welcomed anywhere in the cities of the world, the words were rebranded as infectious parasites.

There was nothing that you could do to stop it. If you had said the First Word then it might take days, weeks or months. But the Last Word always came, and then the speaker always died.

The signs were ripped down from the lamp posts, and with alarm the schools of linguistic theory and etymological ecology were closed. Bricks were thrown, and at least one professor of developmental languages was killed.

The news broadcasts were full of warning. Marie and I took to staying inside during the day. After a while we didn't even bother to turn on the television or listen to the mainstream networks. It was a constant rerun on ignorance.

Officials reported new techniques to tape up your home, to stop the words getting in. Buy new and improved air filter masks for when you have to go out. Chemical sprays that you could use to kill any infestations you had hiding in your gutters.

But no one really knew how they spread. It fast became a sick joke, to try as many different 'cures' as you could. Don't touch them. Don't let them land on you. Kill them on sight. Disinfect yourself. Disinfect them. Don't eat food grown outdoors. Purify your water.

Nothing worked, and after a while everyone just knew that there was nothing that could be done. Somehow the words had gotten in, and I came to suspect that they had always been there, buried deep under the skin or pregnant in our genetics as symbiotic life-forms.

I figure maybe they are like May Bugs, only erupting once every few millennia when the conditions were right. Maybe that's was why half the world went culturally stupid in the Dark Ages, I don't know.

After that first year the city started to eradicate the word-flocks, sending up teams of people with HASMAT suits and chemical sprayers. People weren't allowed outside on cull days, but no matter how hard we taped up the windows and the doors the air was still filled with the acrid tang of toxins.

When that didn't work, the city started quarantining the speakers who had said their First Words. New posters arrived about what number to call if you had seen someone say something they shouldn't. The news broadcasts came to be about how to cope with a speaker in your family, how you can best help them, help yourself, and help society.

No one knew how many people were dying, but it must have been a lot. The streets looked awfully empty these days.

*****

Next morning I was awoken by the bed's cold emptiness.

"Marie?" I croaked frantically, not even pulling on the multiple layers as I stumbled out of the bedroom, ignoring the way my feet stuck to the thin layer of frost on the floorboards. I didn't know what I was going to find, maybe just two words flapping uselessly around our sealed-up apartment, battering to get out.

Instead I found her out in the one-room kitchen and living room, already dressed. Did she look thinner than yesterday? Were those bags under her eyes deeper? "Here." There was a mug of steaming coffee waiting, and a stack of carefully placed bills.

"What's this?" I stammered.

"Get some clothes on you before you catch your death!" She reprimanded, and I knew better than to argue. By the time I came back she was waiting by the door with a rucksack and, beside it the shoebox-nest. "It's our savings. You know that you're always saying that we should get away somehow, get out of the city for a few days…"

"But Marie, the word-"

"Shhh," she said, and her hand shook a little as she patted the shoebox by her side. "Don't… I just think," She took a breath, swallowed. "I think we should release it, somewhere where it's got a chance. I just don't want it to be in the city, you know?"

"But Marie,"

She shook her neon-blue hair and that was the end of it. "I think I've got enough there to rent a car for a few days. If you want, we could head down the coast, south for the summer maybe?"

"Sure" I relented. "Just let me get some things."

"Ha, too late. I've already packed for you." She kicked the singular rucksack.

"Oh, Marie." I said as I grabbed her and folded her into a hug. She hadn't bothered to pack for herself.

We held each other for a long time, until the coffee had grown cold and the tears had stopped.

*****

You have to travel a long way out from the city before you start outrunning the snow, and even then the cold doesn't really let up for miles and miles of frosted roads and heavy grey skies. We took turns driving, daring each other to try and get further than the other, go faster, cover more ground. Neither of us ever said it, but we could almost feel the city itself behind us, its malign influence of chill, concrete and despair.

Sometimes we talked, and when we did I don't think I have ever talked so much in my life. She told me all about her parents, both of whom had been speakers. Marie told me how she missed her mother's knitting and her father's laugh, about every film she'd ever watched, and astonishingly that she liked marsh-mellows but had resigned herself to never buying them because she knew that I didn't.

It felt like we were getting to know each other all over again, she told me about her secret crushes in high school, and I told her mine. We both knew that there would never be another chance.

"We're going to find the right spot," she said, patting the box beside her with her growing First Word. "Where it'll have the best chance of being heard."

Her First Word seemed to be growing every day. God alone knows what it ate, because all it had with it was mangled newspapers and overheard conversation, but by peeking through the air holes we could see it growing bigger, growing luxurious, scintillating wings that looked purple and indigo.

I wanted to know what it said. I wanted Marie to know what it said, before. But she wouldn't let me read it.

"It'll be a surprise." She said, tipping her head and giving the horizon a steady look. "It'll be a present."

Sometimes we would be silent and would watch the white, endless landscape on one side and the choppy grey seas on the other. The cold land around us slowly turned darker and greyer, earthy. We didn't need to say anything during those times, I felt as big as the moon, as big as the air we were driving through.

At night we would crawl into our nest of scavenged blankets and old clothes and generate some warmth in the depths of the car. In the morning we filled the tank with whatever spare gasoline we had, and kept on going. At first Marie asked me to ration the fuel, but I refused. We just filled the tank and figured we work something out when it ran out.

After more than a score of days on the road it was unmistakable. There was a change in the sky, a blush of blue behind the thinning grey, and the air tasted *full*, not cold and dead.

"Sebastian?" Marie said, pulling herself up in her seat and looking around.

It was true. There was green showing against the grey. The wind had stopped, and for once it felt almost warm.

"Over there." She pointed down a smaller road turning, towards a greenish, hazy shape on the southern horizon. "Trees!" We had outrun the cold. "That's where we release it." She said, holding the shoebox with its rustling First Word inside. "It'll have a chance out here."

"Is it time?" I asked, trying to stare into her, into her eyes, judging when the Last Word was going to come.

She shrugged. "I don't know yet, but that looks a good place to me."

I felt a lump in my throat as she spoke. Sometimes that is the best we can ask for.

Deadly Riches

At the back of a beautiful mansion — new but made of exorbitant stone, nonetheless — the guests of the Williams family had gathered around the Olympic-size swimming pool.

"And you should see the wonderful fabric they put on the seats. Oh my lord, it's simply the most luxurious thing you ever touched," said Summer, a painfully attractive twenty-or-so year old woman with radioactive bleached hair. "I couldn't believe when Ashton drove it up the drive and handed me the keys, but I guess I've just been lucky since we shacked up. He's so sweet. Oh, you have to let me show it to you. Don't you think that would be lovely?"

"… Oh. I'm sure we'll have time for that, after dinner," said Abigail Williams. She had been nodding politely and feigning interest for so long that she had failed to realize it was her turn to speak. "But I wouldn't want to be rude to my guests. Maybe Hannah would like to go with you." Abigail stood up as she said that last part, and turned to walk away from the poolside lounge chairs that the three women had been using to bathe in the sun. But she gave her friend, Hannah, a wickedly mischievous smirk as she left, as though to say, 'She's all yours.'

Hannah's tanned face said it all with the look she sent back at Abigail. She was pissed.

"Oh, Hannah, come and take a look, won't you?" Summer said, and Abigail heard Hannah's reply before she walked too far away to hear.

Hannah said, "Summer, is it? We've had a busy day, but I'm sure we can all take a look soon …"

Abigail walked along the edge of the immense swimming pool, with the kids splashing and playing, and hoped she wouldn't get hit with water. She went to a trio of men who were standing and talking some gibber-jabber about cars as well.

"I'm telling you, it's the best," said Ashton. "Since I bought her that car, I've been getting it every —"

"Getting what, little brother?" said Abigail.

"Huh? Nothing," he said, smirking at Howard and Sebastian, who he'd been telling the story to.

"Well, if you're done being a bad influence, I'd like to borrow my husband for a minute. That's okay with you as well, isn't it Howard?" Abigail said.

"Certainly, anything for such old friends, and I do mean *old*," said Howard. "You can tell that by the way this bastard's starting to show some snow on top." He rubbed Sebastian's hair roughly, like someone might do to a big, furry dog, or an old high school pal.

"Thanks a lot," said Sebastian. "Hey, cut it out, or I'll have to show you who's the strongest out of us, again."

Abigail took him by the arm and pulled him away from the other two men, laughing like a good sport. The minute they had gotten around the other side of the poolside sun room, which was currently empty, her true mood revealed itself through her irritated expression. "That *Woman* is driving me crazy, Hannah too — I think she's about ready to slap her."

Sebastian said, "Hannah probably wants to slap just about everyone at one point or another, even you."

"That's not the point. I don't know why Ashton had to bring *her* along. Couldn't he do better than that?" she said.

"I don't know, he's your brother, you know him better than anyone. Could he do better?" Sebastian said. Abigail glared at him. He broke the silence with, "Well, what's wrong with her?"

"What *isn't* wrong with her? Being boring is one thing, and I could excuse that, but she's just so — stupid, and oblivious. Her social manners are severely lacking."

"Well, you've put up with Hannah for all of these years. What's the difference?" he said.

"I'll ask you not to talk about family friends like that, thank you. Besides, you're the one who introduced her to me back in, what was it"

"Must be a decade, but you can blame Howard for that. He's the idiot who married her. But back to the point — why are you telling me about Summer? Your brother's the one who brought her."

"She just won't shut up about her stupid new car that my brother bought her. I just needed to vent and tell someone, you know?"

Sebastian thought for a moment. "How exactly would your brother have gotten enough money to buy a brand-new car? He's always asking for loans. I just answered my own question, didn't I?"

"It's not even a good car. You could by ten of those things if you sold just one of our cars, that's unless you sold one of our *nice* ones," Abigail said.

Sebastian felt a little red around the cheeks. "You loaned him more money. Damn it." He looked at his wife. She was almost ten years his junior, and had the most spectacular set of bright green eyes, not to mention other things. "You're lucky I love you so much, Abigail. You're lucky you're so damned hot, too."

Abigail started to say "Is that so, well I —"

But Howard came around the corner and interrupted them. "Hey, Sebastian, the kids are going to play Marco Polo and they want us to join them. What did you say? Are you up for it, old timer?"

"I'm *one* year older than you, Howard, and yes, I'm ready to defeat you once again," said Sebastian.

"I think I'll sit this one out guys, as I'm sure Hannah's already said as much too," said Abigail.

"Of course. After all, this is a game for men … and children, of course," said Howard. "Come and watch the fun then." He raced back around the corner of the sun room, towards the pool area. Sebastian followed him, stepping quick and eager.

Abigail touched him on the shoulder and stopped him. "Sebastian. You're the lucky one, and don't you forget it, mister," she said, and then started to follow.

"Be careful, Sienna, honey," called Hannah from her lounge chair by the pool.

"I never heard of anyone getting hurt having some fun," said Summer. "Don't worry, Han, just watch your daughter win."

Summer's self-assured tone, and the way she called her 'Han' after having met her just hours prior, must have driven Hannah crazy, Abigail mused. It did give her a little chuckle inside, despite their friendship. But Hannah could probably have been down a peg or two. It might have even made her a little less stand-offish.

"Marco," said Sienna, Hanna and Howard's daughter. She flailed her skinny arms around, hovering near the edge of the shallow end of the pool, where everyone was gathered around.

"Hey, don't go any closer to the deep end!" called Abigail after her own son and daughter. "Delilah, Blake, that's far enough!"

Sienna heard this dead giveaway and hurled herself in what she must have believed was the deep end, where Delilah was apparently trying to hide. But she didn't make it far, especially since she was going in the wrong direction.

"Sienna, stop!" called Howard, who was hovering on his haunches in the water, nearby. But he was not near enough to prevent his daughter from colliding with the rough stone that lined the pool. It matched the house, but it was not the most pragmatic of choices.

Sienna screamed out and opened her eyes the instant she collided into the rough stone. It did not make much difference, however, and her arm quickly began to bleed into the pool. Howard stood up — easily in the shallow end — and ran, or sort of hopped, through the water towards his daughter. "Are you alright? Shit, you had to make your house into a stone castle, didn't you, Seb?" He picked up Sienna and sat her on the edge of the pool."

"Maybe this wasn't the safest of games to play in such a big pool, with kids," shouted Summer. "I'm sure she'll be fine," she said loudly, to no one in particular.

Hannah was running, as well as anyone could with ridiculous high-heeled pool shoes on their feet, around the near end of the pool. She went over to her husband and wounded daughter.

Sebastian got out of the pool and walked over to the frantic parents and child. Sienna was already blubbering, but Sebastian was secretly more concerned about the blood that was trickling down onto his imported stone and starting to join the water inside his pool. "That doesn't look so bad. Sure, the blood makes it seem worse. You're going to be alright, aren't you Sienna"?

"I'm not, I'm not! This is a stupid pool. Ouch! It hurts, mummy!" Sienna wouldn't even look up at Sebastian. She was trying to bury her head into her mother's arm. Hannah was knelt down, awkwardly in such a revealing swimsuit and absurd shoes. The arm that wasn't being used as an emergency pillow by Sienna, was being used to hold the child's wound still for inspection.

Hannah said to Sienna, "You know, I think Uncle Sebastian might be right. Once that bleeding stops, it should be just —"

"He's *not* my uncle, he's just Dad's friend. Ouch, it stings! I need to go to the hospital. Now!" Sienna's face grew an even deeper shade of red, darker than the blood that was running down her arm.

"That's enough," said Howard, and he stood up. "There's no need to be so rude. Hey, Sebastian, can we get this cleaned up and a band aid put on it?"

"Sure thing, pal." He called over to his wife, who was standing in front of her pool chair. "Can we get Ivy to take care of this?"

"Okay. Don't worry!" Abigail called back. She took hold of a little gold disc that was on a chain around her neck. It looked like any ordinary, albeit expensive, piece of jewelry, but when she pressed down in its center, it lit up for a moment. "Ivy will be here any second now. You can time her if you like!"

"Thanks!" said Howard and Sebastian in unison, and they focused their attention back on the bawling child, and her increasingly irritated mother.

Now that the attention was back onto the injured child, Summer, who was standing beside Abigail, said, "What was that you just did? Some sort of pager?"

"Pretty much, yes. Our maid has one just like it, although hers is *fake* gold, of course. "She should be here soon."

"I honestly don't see what the big deal is. Kids cut their self (she didn't say 'themselves') all the time," said Summer. She turned herself around a little, and positioned her pale, firm, bikini-clad behind back on the pool chair she had been sitting on.

Abigail did the same. "I know, but we will never hear the end of it unless we make a big deal. Oh, I didn't say that, *okay*?"

Summer winked at her and said nothing, which surprised Abigail.

Ivy was a thirty-something year old woman who was much more attractive than her stuffy, old-fashioned maid's uniform, and the bags under her eyes, revealed. She appeared at the back door of the house, rushed around the pool to Abigail, and said, "Is there something wrong, Mrs. Williams?" The gold disc around her neck was still flashing red every other second or so, until Abigail pressed the button on her own disc again, and it stopped.

"Sienna's had a little accident, Ivy. Could you please take her and clean it up? Use the guest bathroom downstairs, please," said Abigail from her comfy seat.

"Certainly, Mrs. Williams," said Ivy, and she rushed back around the pool, never actually breaking into a run the whole time, and approached Sebastian, Howard, Hannah, and Sienna. "Come along, dear, let's get that all cleaned up and feeling better." Her voice lightened as she addressed Sienna.

"No!" said Sienna. "Mommy, I'm not going alone with the maid! I won't!"

"Oh, Sienna. I'll come with you, Ivy." said Hannah.

Once the two women had taken the still crying (although the tears seemed rather forced at that point), and barely bleeding, girl inside, Blake said to Sebastian, "Can we still keep playing, Dad? We only just got started."

Delilah joined in, saying, "Yeah, Dad. Can we? Please? Uncle Howard, please? We'll be extra careful."

"I think that's enough of that game, at least until Daddy gets the sides of the pool replaced with something more, safe," said Sebastian to his children. "You two just play in the pool, okay? You can still have a great time without playing that game."

They groaned and tried to look as pathetic as possible, but they didn't argue. Blake, being twelve years old, must have taken the word 'play' as a sign that he should do a cannonball. He ran to the middle of the expansive pool and leapt from the side, creating a respectable splash. Luckily, the sheer size of the pool stopped the displaced water from wetting anyone, or angering them.

"I'm really sorry about all this," said Sebastian to Howard. "You were probably right about choosing something like that for the pool. But I still say it looks great on the house."

"Well, we didn't work to get rich so we could just live in ordinary looking mansions, did we?" said Howard.

"You make a good point," said Sebastian.

And that was when Summer's shrill voice rang out with, "Oh my Gawd! What is wrong with your water? Kids, you have to get out of that pool!"

Sebastian said, "What are you talking about? It's —" and then he noticed what Summer had been yelling about. "What the hell?" The water in his pool had turned several shades darker. It was almost …

"It's going all black!" screamed Delilah, who had been wading around in the shallow end. She scrambled to the steps and started to shake herself. "Mom, I need a towel!"

Once the kids were drying themselves off, everyone — Sebastian, Howard, Abigail, her brother Ashton, his girlfriend Summer, and the two kids — stood with wide eyes and slack jaws, gazing at the blackening water.

"… I have no idea what could be going on," Sebastian said. "This is too much for today, I think. Must be the pH levels or something, I don't know. Say, how about we take this party inside? Honey?"

Abigail stared silently for a moment.

"Abi?" said Sebastian.

"Hey," said Ashton, and he nudged his sister with his elbow.

She widened her eyes and turned her head around, as though trying to figure out who had done it. "What?"

"Shall we send the kids to the games room, and us adults can go to the pool room for some cocktails?" said Sebastian.

"Oh, sure, that sounds like a good idea. I'd like to get away from — whatever *this* thing is doing," and Abigail gestured to the large body of black water. "Can you go and check to see how Sienna's doing, dear?" she said.

"I'll do it," said Howard.

"No, no, you're our guest. You just get to work making us all a round of Mojitos," Sebastian said as he moved inside. "And they had better be good too," he added as he raced inside.

After downing a rather potent cocktail, Abigail started to grow impatient. "I don't know where they could have got to. You'd think Sebastian would have only taken a few minutes to check on a little cut. Honestly." She was sitting at an enormous hardwood bar, which was manned by Howard, busy mixing up another round. Ashton and Summer had helped themselves to some scotch and cola, in addition to their Mojitos.

"Hannah's probably talking his ear off about the dangers of your pool," said Howard. "Don't worry about it. Aren't I good enough company for you, Abi? You've never complained before" He placed his hand on hers from over the bar, and they shared a steamy stare. Ashton and Summer were too busy rifling through the liquor behind the bar to notice.

"Well …" Abigail went googly-eyed like a teenager, then she recollected herself and cleared her throat. "Well, no, no. I should go check. Something could be wrong. I'll be back soon enough," and she winked at Howard and left the room, emphasizing the wiggle in her walk like only a woman with a stiff drink in her can.

Abigail had time enough to sober herself up a little during the walk to the downstairs guest's bathroom; she couldn't shake the feeling that something was seriously wrong, and without Howard there to distract her, or the cocktails, she was worried.

Her pace eventually quickened so that she could barely maintain balance on her showy high-heels (she and Hannah had coordinated equally inefficient footwear for the pool party). She almost slipped a couple of times, but managed to get to the necessary hallway, lined with costly artistic, black and white prints of artistic things like trees and shadows of birds. And then she could hear erratic voices, which might have been her husband, and Sienna?

"Honey? Is something wrong, I —" and she blood-screamed this next word: "Ivy!" The fair maid was lying inside the bathroom, near the doorway, her throat sliced open and blood spreading out on the white tiles around her neck. "My God!" She looked over the body, to the right of the rectangular guest's bathroom, much smaller than the main bathroom. Sebastian was there, and he had hold of Sienna's wrists. Sienna was — growling, was the only word to describe it. She had hold of a pair of scissors, the ones from the first aid kit.

Sebastian was struggling more than a grown man should have been to keep hold of an eleven year old girl. He looked over at Abigail quickly, trying not to get distracted. "Abi! Go get Howard, call for an ambulance, and the police," he grunted the words, still struggling as he was to avoid the red-smeared scissors. They were the big, expensive kind, of course; the type that could remove a finger or two.

"Sienna, what are you doing? Stop it!" Abigail said. She almost stuttered and the words came out sharp and breathy. Abigail stepped past the dead maid, avoided putting her shoes in the blood, and tried not to look down, without actually shutting her eyes. "Stop it!" she cried at the back of the girl. She could not see her face, and was afraid that she might turn on her.

"No, Abigail," Sebastian said when he looked up and saw that his wife had entered the bathroom. "Get help — now!"

Abigail did not argue, but turned and shuffled off, her heels clacking the tiles. She picked up the pace the moment she was clear of the sleek surface, and disappeared out of the door.

That left Sebastian, Sienna, and the corpse of Ivy. Sienna still had not said anything to him, but he spoke to her, in their struggle. "Sienna, why are you doing this? What's wrong with you?" was all he could think to say. It sounded weak to him.

"I've always hated you," she said. "And I hate that stupid, poor maid. I never wanted to come here. My Daddy hates you!" Her voice tangled around his brain. That was not the voice of a little girl. Sure, the tone was right, even the way the words formed. But there was so much — hatred, dead, void of human life, but still so *hateful*. And her eyes — they were completely black, not a spot of white, or their usual blue centers.

"What the fuck happened to you?" he said. His heart shot up to double its pace, and adrenaline took over. Sebastian stepped back to brace his foot against something, the toilet. He yanked the girl's arm upward, trying to make her loose the scissors.

A cracked scream shot out through Sienna's lips, opened wide and spitting as she belted his ears with the most unnerving sound Sebastian had ever endured. Sienna kicked at him, catching his stomach, and hoisted herself backward to free her arms. She snarled and Sebastian let go of her arms, letting her fall.

The girl drove herself back, unable to stop the momentum her kick had created. With a brittle crack, her head shot through the glass of the little guest shower. Her body didn't fall to the floor.

Sebastian stood, his chest almost turning itself inside out with his efforts to catch his breath. He could not comprehend the scene before him; his pretty and courteous maid of six years, her throat slashed, bleeding onto the bathroom tiles; the only child of his best friend, hung up on the broken shower screen glass, stuck like a dead fish.

It was too much, and the fully grown man ran from that bathroom like a child who had seen a big spider. He slammed the door shut and stopped, leaning against it, to finish catching his breath. He checked himself for cuts, but there wasn't so much as a nick, or a drop of blood on his hands or anywhere else.

He took off down the hallway and came to a stop when he saw a broken bit of, plastic? It was a little tube that looked snapped at one end. The heel of a shoe! He thought of the ridiculous high heels his wife had been trying to run with, and loped around the corner of the hallway.

Sure enough, there was Abigail, cast across the hard wood floor, limbs about her, revealing the intensity of her fall. He quickly crouched down beside her. "Abi? Abigail? Talk to me, honey, please." He noticed a mean dent in the lower wall, near here head; it was shallow, but the walls were hard as cash could buy.

He put his hand on her neck, trying to feel for a pulse, but he was not getting one. Something touched him on the shoulder and he could have jumped through the roof from the shock.

"What —" he turned his head enough to see Ivy standing behind him, holding the hefty pair of scissors that had been used to slit her own throat minutes earlier. Sebastian turned his body and half-fell, half-sprung, trying to move himself away from the maid.

"You rich pig. Think you're better than me. And you're useless whore wife. You know I've spat in every meal she's ever had me make?" He said,with the same dead, hateful tone, and black eyes as Sienna. Sebastian thought he must be asleep, or losing his mind. What if this was all in his head? What if he had gone psychotic and done all this himself?

While the maid was telling him what she really thought, he used the chance to stand up and move away from Ivy, and the twin steel blade in her hand. The blood no longer flowed from her neck wound, but it stuck all over her blouse.

Ivy rushed toward him with the scissors raised like an ice pick. She chortled — actually smiled as well — and brought the scissors down at him.

Sebastian didn't hesitate at all this time, not like he had done with Sienna. He stepped aside and out of the way, which was easy enough; Ivy was too far gone with hatred to display any grace. She bolted by him, and he followed her with a shove. The maid toppled forward and landed face down. But she quickly pushed herself back up and was standing again.

"I've dreamed of killing you so many times, you have no idea," she said. "You're spoiled little brats too. You're nothing but a disease, you should be cut out." Ivy growled the words as she lunged at Sebastian again. This time she caught his upper arm, on the right side, as he tried to grab her wrist.

The cut was not much, but deep enough to shock Sebastian. He reacted by kicking, bringing his foot out and downward on the bloodied woman's knee. There was a snap, but she did not scream. Sebastian pushed her back, all the while with her slashing at him with the scissors.

Ivy stumbled backwards, cackling like a witch, and then as she put the injured leg down, there was another snap — a spine-tingling sound, and bone jutted out through the side of her leg. She fell to the floor, still trying to drag herself to Sebastian.

All he could think of was his Abigail. He turned to the corner of the hall and saw nothing other than a dent in the wall, but his wife was gone.

The murderous voice of his maid followed him with threats and promises of death as he ran back down the hallway, past the bathroom where this killing had begun, and he headed to the games room.

Sebastian moved toward the center of the house. Abigail must have … gotten back up; he couldn't bring himself to think about how she might look and act. He moved quickly through the large central dining area, which was flanked by double doors on all sides. They were usually kept closed, and only one was now open, leading toward the stairs, and the bedroom. Could Abigail have gone that way? Did he want to find her?

No. But the kids … *They're in the games room*, he told himself internally. And he hoped to God, or whoever was doing this, that Blake and Delilah were still alright. Sebastian made his decision, ignored the open twin doors to the stairs, and headed through the ones to the left of them.

The games room was on the other side of the house, sharing a wall with the pool area. At least he was headed away from Ivy, and he did not encounter anyone else as he moved. The silence amplified his footsteps, making Sebastian cringe with each of them. He had no intentions of coming across any more … dead.

When he came to the big door that leads into the games room, although it was more the size of a hall really, he stopped, took a breath, and turned the handle.

"Blake? Delilah?" He walked tentatively into the room. He couldn't hear anyone. The excessively big flat screen TV displayed a video game. Whoever had been playing; their character was being shot by virtual assailants. The image flashed red with each bullet hit. The sounds of grunts and gunshots from the game jarred Sebastian's frail nerves.

"Kids? Are you —"

"Hello, Daddy." That was Delilah's voice. Sebastian spun his head around and took in a panoramic view of the room. He couldn't see her. Out from under the foosball table crawled Delilah. *No blood*, Sebastian thought, feeling relief. "You know something?" she said.

"What? Are you okay? Where's your brother?"

"He hated you anyway. It's okay, he's with us now too," said his eight year old daughter as she stood up before the soccer game. The eyes were black, like the others' had been. She brought her hand in front of her and showed a kitchen knife, clean. "I hate you too. But that's not why I have to kill you. It wants you to join us. You'll like it," she said in a matter-of-fact way.

"Delilah, no ..." he couldn't fathom the energy to react. Sebastian felt like just curling up on the floor and weeping, but he thought about Blake. He couldn't see the boy. Maybe his son was still alive, maybe this thing, his daughter, was lying. *I can still save him*, he thought.

"Give me a hug, Daddy. Why don't you ever have time for me?" Delilah said as she stepped forward, quickly, and slashed at her father with the knife that had been used to cut the very occasional Sunday roast. It tore his shirt and bit into his skin, but he could not react.

"You're a terrible father, aren't you?" Delilah said — or whatever was inside her body — as she unleashed a flurry of small, child-like motions. Sebastian felt the blade a few more times, and his eyes were watery.

"No!" he suddenly yelled. "You're not my daughter! What are you!?"

The girl giggled with glee as Sebastian pushed her away from him.

"We're your children," came another voice, a boy. Sebastian stepped back from the girl and looked over to see Blake. He was standing over by the little lounge that was printed with pictures of trucks and motorcycles. He was free from blood or injury too, at a look, but how?

The black water, Sebastian thought. He didn't stay to think any longer though. Delilah came at him with the knife again, but he turned and ran out the door, slamming it behind. The children screamed after him, but he blocked out whatever they were saying, and raced toward the stairs.

This time, moving in the direction of the main area of the giant house, Sebastian heard clattering and screams. Some of the voices seemed human, and familiar, but they were mingled with inhuman cries of hatred.

Sebastian thanked the universe when he made it to the stairs without coming by the sources of those screams. He moved as fast as a nearly middle-aged business man was able, for the children could have followed. The thought of facing Blake and Delilah again made his heart ache.

Without knowing why, he headed for the master bedroom, which he and Abigail had shared for years, taking three steps at once. It was getting hard to breath, and his slothful heart struggled to pump as fast as it was being asked to. The only hope left for Sebastian lied in the image of his wife's face, her eyes still bright green and lovely as ever. *She's still herself, still alive,* he thought over and over and he ascended the stairs and ran down to his bedroom.

Sebastian booted the door open, for it was slightly ajar, and he no longer cared about subtlety. His vision was marred with hot tears and his heart was painfully throbbing. Limbs tingling, he stepped into the middle of the magnificent bedroom. There was the bed, draped with the luxurious curtains that had kept nights so warm and safe. He and his wife embraced in each other's arms.

"Abigail?" he said, and pulled the bed curtain aside. There she was, lying on her back like some sleeping beauty. She did not respond, but her soft breasts slowly rose and fell beneath her swimsuit.

"Abi!" It was the happiest Sebastian had ever been, but at the same time it was the most terrified he'd felt. Then her eyes opened, bright green.

"What's going on?" she said. "My head … I broke my heel, fell." The words were shattered. Her eyes did not easily focus on her husband. He sat by her side on their marital bed.

"Abi, I, it's all wrong. I'm so sorry …"

"Sebastian? It's not your fault … I love you …" and she closed her eyes.

"Abi? Abigail? Don't close your eyes. Stay awake." But her chest had ceased to move.

Sebastian heard movement from downstairs, and the thump, thump, of things on the steps, perhaps at the top of them by now. He had been too distracted with his wife's' death … *Oh, Abigail* … he thought, and began to openly cry.

The bedroom door was mostly open, but something smacked into it.

Thud.

And again.

Thud.

Footsteps now sounded inside the room. Sebastian stood up and moved his head around the bed curtain. It was Blake, Delilah … Howard moved in behind them, and Hannah. Ashton and his girlfriend, Summer, were behind. They were all — gone, the blood was obvious from across the room. Sebastian could see the intent in their movements, the hate in their expressions, and the blackness in their eyes.

Something grabbed his arm. He froze to the spot.

"I never did love you," came Abigail's voice from the bed. He didn't even turn to look at her. She said, "I've cheated on you since we met. You're such a worthless idiot."

"We've been fucking since you got married. Fucking loser," said Howard.

Sebastian died with nothing but contempt surrounding him, his eyes closed. He tried to be somewhere else, tried to make himself wake up. It didn't even hurt after a while, once he hit the floor, after the first dozen kicks to his head, and the blood was flowing freely from his body. But surely, he would return soon …